CRACKING THE MAGIKARP CODE

CRACKING THE MAGIKARP CODE

UNOFFICIAL ADVENTURES FOR POKÉMON GO PLAYERS

Book Four

Alex Polan

Sky Pony Press
New York

Copyright © 2016 by Hollan Publishing, Inc.

First Edition

This is a work of fiction. Names, characters, places, and incidents are from the author's imagination, and used fictitiously.

Sky Pony Press books may be purchased in bulk at special discounts for sales promotion, corporate gifts, fund-raising, or educational purposes. Special editions can also be created to specifications. For details, contact the Special Sales Department, Sky Pony Press, 307 West 36th Street, 11th Floor, New York, NY 10018 or info@skyhorsepublishing.com.

Sky Pony® is a registered trademark of Skyhorse Publishing, Inc.®, a Delaware corporation.

Visit our website at www.skyponypress.com.

Books, authors, and more at SkyPonyPressBlog.com.

10 9 8 7 6 5 4 3 2 1

Library of Congress Cataloging-in-Publication Data is available on file.

Special thanks to Erin L. Falligant.

Cover illustration by Jarrett Williams
Cover colors by Jeremy Lawson
Cover design by Brian Peterson

Print ISBN: 978-1-5107-2205-7
Ebook ISBN: 978-1-5107-2207-1

Printed in Canada

CHAPTER 1

"**H**as anyone seen my open-house handouts?" Mom's voice rang out from down the hall. Ethan said nothing. He was staring at the handouts—or what used to be the handouts. Now they were just a pile of shredded paper beneath the dining room table. And Mystic, Ethan's new Chow Chow puppy, sat beside the heap, looking pretty proud of her mess.

"Uh-oh, what did Miss Misty do this time?" asked his younger sister Devin as she stepped into the dining room.

"Don't call her that," Ethan snapped for what felt like the hundredth time. "Her name is Mystic, like Team Mystic—our Pokémon GO team. That's what we said we would call her, remember?" He reached down to pick up the puppy, but she shimmied out of his grasp and waddled over to Devin instead, like she'd been doing all morning.

"She's too cute for just one name," said Devin, scooping the furry puppy into her arms. "We could call her Cinnamon because her fur is so red. Or Eevee because she has a fluffy mane and bushy tail like that cute little Pokémon."

"No," said Ethan, "Eevee's ears are way too big. I think Mystic looks more like Growlithe. They both have little pointy ears that poke through the mane of fur at their neck. And they're both orange—I mean, except for Growlithe's stripes."

"Fine," said Devin, kissing Mystic on the nose. "One of her nicknames can be 'Growlithe,' especially when she growls." She gave the pup a stern look. "But don't you go evolving into a full-grown Arcanine anytime soon!"

They heard the clatter of plates in the kitchen, which meant Dad was about to call them in for breakfast.

"C'mon, let's clean this up, quick," said Ethan, scooping up the shreds of paper.

"Clean up what?" Dad poked his bald head through the swinging door. "Uh-oh. First, my shoes. Then the living room pillows. Now this. Has your mother seen it yet?"

Ethan shook his head.

"Bad girl," said Dad, waving a plastic spatula at Mystic. But she paid him about as much attention as she paid Ethan. She wagged her tail and chewed up another piece of paper right by Dad's foot.

When they heard the sound of Mom's heels on the kitchen floor, everyone froze.

"Misty, get that paper out of your mouth!" Devin whispered, tugging on the paper scrap.

But Mystic thought Devin wanted to play tug-of-war. As Mom stepped into the room, the puppy had just ripped the paper out of Devin's fingers and was growling, shaking its prize in the air.

"Oh, no," said Mom, her jaw dropping. "No, no, no! The open house starts in half an hour!"

"I can help you print more flyers," Ethan offered. But he knew it would take longer than half an hour to replace what Mystic had chewed up in less than a minute.

"We were just coming up with nicknames for her," said Devin in a bright voice. "What do you think of Growlithe?" She was pretty good at changing the subject whenever Mystic—or anyone else—got in trouble.

Mom sighed and squatted down to gather the

shredded flyers. "I think we should call her Chew Chew, because she's a very *naughty* little Chow Chow."

Mystic whined and rolled on her back beside Mom.

"Wow, she really listens to you," said Ethan. "How come she ignores me?"

Mom shrugged. "Give her time. She'll come around, as long as you're firm with her—and do not let her chew on anything except her toys."

She pulled a tiny tennis ball out of a basket on the floor and rolled it to Mystic, who bounded up to it and grabbed it. It stuck out of the front of her mouth like a tiny yellow pacifier.

"Should we take her to the dog park?" asked Dad. "It's right next to the lake!" He was off work this last week of summer, which meant fishing at the lake—one of Dad's favorite things. He was grinning like a little kid just talking about it.

Mom hesitated. "Can you keep Mystic on the leash and *out* of the lake?" she asked, looking from Dad to Ethan to Devin and back again.

"Yes!" said Ethan. He was pretty excited about the lake, too. He'd heard it was crawling with Water-type Pokémon.

"It's going to be up to you two to keep an eye on the puppy," said Mom. "Because your dad is trying to catch the big one this year." She winked at Dad.

"I'm not *trying*," he argued. "I'm *going* to. This is the year!" He waved his spatula in the air to accentuate the point.

Ethan laughed. Every year, Dad claimed he was going to catch the big one—the four-foot-long Northern Pike that he'd seen one summer on the end of his line, and then lost. And every year, he came home with a gazillion pan fish instead. Mom would fry them up, and they'd enjoy a dinner of crispy little fish while Dad talked about the one that got away.

Fishing week was tradition—the official end to summer. And this year, Ethan hoped he'd catch the big one, too—a Kingler or Tentacool or Gyarados. Something new and different. Something *powerful*.

"We'll keep an eye on Mystic," he promised his mom. "And we'll make sure Dad wears sunscreen, too."

Mom grinned. "Thank you, Ethan. Your sister, too. We have to protect the redheads in this family."

Devin laughed and gave Mystic a hug. "That includes you, Cinnamon. You take after Dad, just like I do."

Ethan cringed. *Enough with the nicknames!* he

wanted to say. But he let it go this time. There was too much to do before heading off to the lake. First thing to do? Charge my phone! he thought as he raced to his room.

He wasn't going to catch the big one with a dead battery!

"PokéStop!" announced Devin as they tumbled out of Dad's car after Mystic.

The informational sign at the edge of the parking lot showed a huge map of the lake. And as Ethan spun the photo of the map on his phone, he collected two Poké Balls and some Potion.

But as soon as they past the map, they ran into another sign: No DOGS ALLOWED ON THE BEACH OR IN THE PICNIC AREA.

"Wow, there are sure a lot of rules about dogs," said Ethan, gesturing toward the sign. "There are more places we *can't* go than places we *can*!"

Dad barely noticed that Ethan and Devin had stopped. He was walking ahead toward the beach, whistling and swinging his tackle box. Mystic strained at her leash, trying to follow.

"Dad, we can't go that way!" called Ethan, gently guiding the pup back. "We'll take Mystic to the dog park and then meet you at the lake—the non-beach part, at least."

"What, huh?" asked Dad, nearly losing his hat as he spun around. "Okay, sure. We'll see you soon."

Devin shook her head. "He's already dreaming about the big one," she said, laughing. "I sure hope he gets it this year."

"Yeah," said Ethan, "but if he does, I'm going to miss those crispy little pan fish."

He drooled just thinking about them as he followed the fork in the trail toward the dog park. There were even *more* signs there about cleaning up after your dogs and keeping them on leashes when they weren't in the water.

And there were plenty of dogs, too. Mystic stopped to greet a Dachshund, which was long and low to the ground. She sniffed the backside of a Basset Hound. And she growled at a Greyhound that was three times her size.

"What a cute Chow!" said the Greyhound's owner, a woman with her hair in a messy bun. But when her son reached out to pet Mystic, the puppy shrank back against Devin's legs.

"She's not so sure about strangers," Ethan tried to explain. What he really wanted to say was, *She's not so sure about boys.* But he was still hoping Mom was wrong about that.

As Mystic led them away from the little boy, Ethan noticed the dogs' swimming area. A long dock stretched out into the lake, and beside it, two Labrador retrievers—one yellow and one chocolate colored—paddled toward shore. The Chocolate Lab had a tennis ball in its mouth.

Mystic honed right in on that tennis ball. She gave a squeaky little bark and then promptly bolted. The leash slid from his hand, and Mystic took off running—straight toward the lake.

CHAPTER 2

"**M**ystic, stop!"

Ethan raced after the dog. He was relieved when she stopped just short of the water lapping against the muddy shore. But as the Chocolate Lab with the tennis ball loped out of the water, Mystic went straight for his ball.

Growling and crouching, she yapped at the dog. He turned in annoyed circles, trying to avoid her. Finally, he growled back and lunged at Mystic.

"No!" cried Devin. "He's going to hurt her!"

"No he won't." A kid with a blonde buzz cut and bright orange swim trunks jumped up from his beach towel and ran over. "He won't hurt her," he said again, sounding just as annoyed as his dog. "He just doesn't want to share his ball."

He clipped a leash to the Lab's collar and led him toward the towel. Mystic started to follow, until Devin called out, "Misty, stop!"

This time, the puppy listened. She trotted toward Devin as if to say, "Hey! Long time no see, buddy."

Then the other Lab—the yellow one—waded out of the lake. Ethan could see what was coming from a mile away, but he couldn't move!

Sure enough, the dog braced her body and then shook it, sending off a great muddy spray.

Ethan took most of it in the face. "Ew."

"Sorry!" called a teenage girl who had been sitting on the pier. "Bad girl, Sandy." She pulled her long, brown hair into a ponytail and then grabbed the towel that was draped over the post of the pier. She offered it to Ethan. "Here, use this before I dry her off."

"A towel would have been a good idea," said Devin, lifting up Mystic's muddy paws one by one. "Mom's not going to be happy."

"A tennis ball would have been a good idea, too," said Ethan as he handed the towel back to the girl. "We should have brought Mystic's— our dog's—ball so that she wouldn't try to steal someone else's! Sorry about that."

"No problem," said the girl. She smiled and then squatted and began drying off her dog.

Ethan and Devin led Mystic away from the pier and back up the trail. Then they hurried past the beach and picnic area. Families were already cooking hot dogs, which made Mystic's nose go crazy. She tugged at her leash, but Devin held her back. "You're not allowed there, sweetie," she said. "Sorry."

As they neared the quieter end of the lake, Devin gave Mystic some slack in her leash—just enough so that she could run ahead a few feet.

While Mystic followed her nose, rustling up birds, butterflies, and ducks from the grasses near the water, Ethan and Devin started rustling up Pokémon on their phones: Staryu, Venonat, Krabby, Poliwag, and even a giant, flopping Magikarp. They took turns, one holding Mystic's leash and the other catching Pokémon.

"It's like Mystic can smell them or something," said Devin. "Her nose works better than the Pokémon GO tracker. She's leading us right to them!"

Ethan knew that wasn't possible, but it *did* seem like wherever Mystic found some bird or animal to hunt, they found Pokémon, too. *Now, if only I could catch them*, he thought as he flung a Poké Ball toward a Goldeen—and missed.

"I need to work on my throws," he told Devin. "I'm not going to get Great Balls until I hit Level Twelve, and at this rate, that'll take forever." It had taken him weeks just to reach Level Nine.

"Gia could teach you how to throw better," said Devin as she bent to unwind the leash from around Mystic's leg.

Ethan had already thought of asking their friend and teammate for some pointers. Gianna scored extra points for great and excellent throws all the time, and she was the only one of them who had mastered the curveball, too.

"Hey, if we come back to the lake tomorrow, we should ask Dad if Gia and Carlo can come, too," he said. Gianna's older brother, Carlo, was a Level-Fifteen Trainer. With Gianna and Carlo's help, Ethan would hit Level Ten before the week ended!

"Let's go ask him right now," said Devin.

They found Dad fishing near a willow tree that bent low over the water. Or was he sleeping? His hat had slid down over his eyes.

As they got closer, Ethan saw that Dad's eyes were open wide. He was studying his phone.

"Hey, Dad, are you playing Pokémon GO?" Ethan called to him.

"What? No," said Dad, straightening up. "I'm fishing. I just thought I'd, you know, catch a Larry or two while I waited for some action on the line."

"Larry" was Dad's pet name for Weedle and, for some reason, he caught an awful lot of them.

Ethan grinned at Devin. Dad liked playing Pokémon GO as much as he and Devin did. But he'd never admit it—at least not in front of Mom.

"Um, Dad?" said Devin.

"Yeah?"

"You might want to check your bobber."

Ethan looked, too, and saw it bobbing up and down like a Poké Ball with a Magikarp trapped inside.

Dad grabbed his hat and jumped up. He yanked his pole up from the log he'd propped it against and started reeling. "Oh, it's a big one," he said. "I can feel it! Hold on, kids!"

He braced his legs against the shore as if he were reeling in a Great White Shark. Mystic barked and growled as if she were going to take on that shark herself.

Finally, the fish sprang from the water. But what was dangling from Dad's line wasn't exactly the big one.

Ethan cleared his throat. "Hmm. I wonder why they call those little fish Bluegill when they're actually kind of yellow?"

When Dad didn't respond, Devin added, "Well, I do like crispy little fish!"

"Me, too," boomed a voice behind them. A man with a shock of white hair tipped his fishing hat toward them as he passed. He held up a line of fish he'd caught, which had plenty of Bluegill hanging from it. But there were a few really big fish on there, too, Ethan noticed.

"I'm going to go home now and leave a few in the lake for you." The old man grinned and gave one last wave as he walked toward the parking lot, his tackle box bouncing against his side.

"Where'd he catch those big fish?" asked Ethan.

"Probably at the bridge," said Dad, pointing toward a wooden bridge that arched over the stream running into the lake. "Badfish Creek Bridge. I'd fish over there, too, if it weren't always so crowded."

"Badfish?" asked Ethan. "Why would anyone want to fish in a creek with bad fish in it?"

"I don't know," said Devin. "But the bridge is also a Pokémon gym. Look!" She held up her phone, which showed a towering, yellow Team Instinct gym.

"Cool!" Ethan pulled out his own phone, being careful to keep a tight grip on Mystic's leash. He chuckled when he saw the Pokémon spinning on top. "Magikarp? The Gym Leader there fights with a floppy Magikarp?"

"Yeah—that's even his Trainer name, see? *MagikarpKid*. And he's the only Defender at the gym right now. Hey, we should try to take it over!" said Devin. "We haven't battled or trained our Pokémon at Dottie's in ages."

It was true. Ethan could barely remember the last time he, Devin, Carlo, and Gianna had met at Dottie's Doughnuts, their favorite Team Mystic gym. They hadn't battled at any gym, not even the one they'd taken over at the library last month.

"Not since we got Mystic," he said, bending over to scratch the Chow's furry head. "We've been kind of busy since then."

"Let's do it," said Devin. "Dad can watch Mystic while we battle."

Dad held out his hand for the leash. "I might as well puppy-sit," he said. "Since the fishing thing isn't exactly *panning out*." Then he cracked up, as if he'd just told the world's funniest joke.

"Get it?" said Dad. "Pan fish?"

Ethan just shook his head. He'd learned a long time ago not to encourage Dad's bad jokes. They only got worse when he did.

He made sure Mystic's leash was wrapped snugly

around Dad's wrist. Then he followed Devin past the boat launch toward the bridge. They sat on a large flat rock by the water. Then he tapped on the gym on his phone screen and selected his Pokémon for battle.

"Let's see," said Ethan, "I'm going to lead with Vaporeon. That's my toughest Pokémon now." He also threw in Drowzee, his *newest* Pokémon, just for fun. Then he rounded out his team of six with a few more powerful Pokémon.

When he saw sparks fly from the top of the tower, he realized Devin was already battling. "Hey, wait for me!"

Pretty soon, he was tapping the screen, too, attacking the flopping Magikarp. He filled the blue bar at the top of his screen quickly. Then he held his finger down to release Vaporeon's Water Pulse attack.

"Again, Vaporeon," he ordered. "Destroy that dirty carp!"

He delivered Water Pulse twice, and then a third time.

And then the battle was over—almost too soon.

"We did it!" said Devin. "Team Mystic takes control. Which Pokémon are you leaving here?"

"Drowzee," said Ethan while he healed his Vaporeon. "Because that battle almost put me to sleep."

Devin rolled her eyes. "And that was a total Dad joke."

Ethan glanced over his shoulder to see if Dad was watching them, but he seemed to be playing his own game of Pokémon GO—one-handed, while the other hand kept Mystic under control. Dad's fishing line was still in the water, but it didn't seem to be getting much action.

Then something caught Ethan's eye in the lake below. "Duck!" he said, nudging Devin. The duck dove underwater. It was apparently fishing, too.

"Duck butt," said Devin, giggling at the cute tail feathers poking out of the water.

A sharp bark rang out, which meant that Mystic had her eye on that duck butt, too. When the duck resurfaced and swam a little too close to shore, Ethan cupped his hand over his mouth and called out a warning.

"Dad, hang on tight to . . ."

Too late. Ethan saw the look of horror on Dad's face as he looked down at his open hand—that hand that seconds ago had held the dog leash.

Mystic yapped and ran alongshore beside the squawking, flapping duck. Her leash bounced along the ground behind her.

"Grab it!" Ethan called to Devin, who was

running toward her already. "Step on the leash!"

She tried, but tripped. Devin face-planted in a spray of reeds, and Ethan tore past her, his eyes fixed on Mystic.

As the duck flapped its wings and finally rose into the air, Mystic stood up on her hind legs. Ethan saw his opportunity and dove for the leash.

But Mystic had already moved on. The leash slipped out of reach.

Ethan pushed himself to his feet, scanning the shoreline for the dog. Where had she gone?

There she was, rolling on her back with her feet in the air. Ethan couldn't help laughing. "Are you scratching your back?" he whispered, as he snuck up on the puppy and grabbed the end of her leash. "Does that feel good?"

That's when the stench hit him.

Mystic wasn't rolling on the ground because it felt good. Mystic was rolling in something.

Something dead.

And something very fishy.

CHAPTER 3

"Ugh," said Devin, pinching her nose. "What *is* that?"

"That," said Dad, "would be a carp. A very big, very dead carp."

"A Magikarp?" Devin asked, her voice coming out all nasally from beneath her fingertips.

"No, there's nothing magical about that carp," said Ethan, trying to pull Mystic away from the dead fish.

"They're fun to try to catch, though," said Dad. "Carp put up quite a fight. Just like the Northern Pike I saw that summer." His eyes glazed over, as if he were back on that boat, still reeling in the big one.

"Dad, snap out of it," said Ethan quickly. "Mystic is going to need a serious bath. We should go home."

But Mystic wasn't going anywhere—at least not with Ethan. She tugged harder in the other direction, back toward that dead fish.

"Here, let me try," said Devin, reaching for the leash.

Good luck, he thought as he handed it over.

"Mystic, *come*," said Devin, sounding an awful lot like Mom. And sure enough, that puppy followed her.

Ethan sighed and fell back in step with Dad, who was gathering his gear. In the sunlight, he could see that Dad had gotten sunburned—at least across the bottom half of his face, which the brim of his hat hadn't been covering.

And Ethan was feeling a little burned, too. *I'm the one who wanted the puppy!* he wanted to holler at Devin's back. *So why does she like you better?*

Gianna crouched beside Mystic, letting the puppy sniff her hand. Mystic looked up at Gianna warily, as if to say, "Now who are you again?"

Maybe it's because of Gia's bug cap, thought Ethan with a smile. Gianna wore the cap any time they went Pokémon hunting. She thought the antennae on top brought her good luck, especially when it came to catching Bug-type Pokémon.

When she bent over, Mystic raised a tentative paw and batted at one of the antennae, which made Gianna giggle. That made the antennae bounce. And Mystic raised her rump in the air and growled at it.

Carlo grinned and shook his head. "She's pretty cute. So, was your mom mad about the rolling-in-the-dead-fish thing?"

"Nope," said Ethan. "Mom didn't even know about that. We gave Mystic a bath before Mom got home from work. And when she asked if Mystic got lots of exercise at the dog park, we said yes. Because that was true. It's a lot of work chasing ducks and rolling in dead fish, right?"

"Right," said Carlo, wrinkling up his nose.

Gianna laughed. "Carlo's not big on fish, but I *love* fishing. Does your dad have extra poles?" She looked hopefully toward the willow tree, where Dad had set up shop again.

"Don't even think about it," said Carlo in his big brother voice. "We're not here to fish, Gia. We're here to catch Pokémon. Like the Voltorb that's sitting on your foot right now."

Ethan pulled out his phone, too. "I don't even know what a Voltorb is," he said. "Oh! It looks like a giant Poké Ball. An angry one!"

"Or a giant fishing bobber," said Gianna, staring over his shoulder.

"Give it up, Gia," said Carlo. "We're not going fishing!"

She crossed her arms. "Fine. Then can I borrow your phone to catch the Voltorb?"

Gianna was the only one of the four who didn't have her own phone. Her mom was making her wait till she turned ten—which would be next year. But Ethan could tell that the wait was just about killing her.

Carlo sighed. "Sure."

But he forgot to sign out first. So after Gianna caught the Voltorb, she said, "Hey, you have enough Voltorb candy to evolve it. Can we?"

"Wait!" said Carlo, snatching the phone back. "Let me do it."

Ethan and the girls all crowded in to watch Voltorb evolve on Carlo's phone. The Poké-Ball–like Pokémon was sucked into the big ball of light, spun around, and emerged as . . .

A grinning, eyebrow-waggling Electrode!

Ethan laughed out loud. "That looks like Dad!"

he joked. "The bottom half of its face is sunburned red, and the top is white as a ghost."

They all glanced at Dad, who sitting in the shade of the willow tree, protecting his half-sun-burned face. When he saw them staring, he grinned and waved, looking an awful lot like the Pokémon on Carlo's screen.

Devin covered her mouth, hiding a smile. "Poor Dad. I sure hope this is the year he catches the big one."

"Me, too," said Ethan.

"So where's this gym you guys were talking about?" asked Carlo, spinning the map around on his phone. "Over there by the bridge?" He shaded his eyes against the morning sun.

"Yeah," said Devin, pulling up the gym on her own phone. "Oh, look, the Magikarp kid is back!"

"Really?" said Ethan. "I thought we took care of him yesterday." But there was that ugly Magikarp again, flopping around at the top of the gym. His Combat Power was a lot higher today, too. "Should we fight him together, now that we're all here?"

"I wish I had a phone," complained Gianna, kicking at the ground with her shoe.

"Here, use mine," said Devin sweetly. "You're a better fighter, and besides, I have to keep an eye on Misty."

"Wait, who's Misty?" asked Gianna, her eyebrows scrunched together.

Ethan shook his head. "Never mind," he said, hoping Gianna wouldn't pick up the nickname and start using it, too. "Just get logged in, Giadude99, and let's get closer to the bridge so we can take down this gym!"

Giadude99 was Gianna's Trainer name. And with her and Carlo—or Carlozard14—battling beside Ethan, that Magikarp didn't stand a chance.

Pretty soon, the Badfish Creek Bridge gym was Team Mystic blue. And Carlo was the new Gym Leader.

"You left your Electrode at the gym?" asked Gianna, laughing.

"Yes!" he said. "For Ethan and Devin's dad. Maybe Electrode, the giant, sunburned fishing bobber, will bring him good luck."

Ethan was checking out the Electrode on his phone when something floated by in the breeze—a scrap of paper. And then another.

"Hey, is someone littering, or what?" he asked.

"Uh-oh," said Devin, whirling around. "Mystic!"

Ethan's eyes followed the leash from her hand to the puppy on the other end, who had found a piece of paper on the ground and was ripping it to shreds.

Gianna picked up a scrap and studied the blue and green swirls. "No big deal," she said. "I think it's just an old fishing map. See? These lines show how deep the water is in different parts of the lake."

Carlo held up a piece, too. "But there's handwriting on it, too—see? The red ink marks look like some sort of symbols. Are those fish?"

Ethan tilted his head sideways to look at the symbols. They were ovals with little triangles on the end, like fishtails. "Yeah," he said. "That piece has two fish drawn on it."

"This one has three," said Devin, holding up a triangular piece of paper. "What do you think it means?"

"It's like a secret code," said Ethan. "A fish code. The Magikarp Code!"

Gianna's eyes lit up. "Ooh, I'll bet Team Mystic can crack it! We're good at solving mysteries."

"Yes!" agreed Devin. "If we put the pieces together, maybe we can figure it out."

Pretty soon, all four of them were on the ground, sliding pieces sideways and spinning them around to try to make them fit. As Ethan slid a piece next to Devin's and watched the lines match up, he felt a shiver of excitement. "That's a match!" he said. "Those three fish are drawn next to this marshy area—a good place for fish to hide, maybe?"

"Are you thinking what I'm thinking?" asked Carlo, studying the map.

Ethan nodded. "Someone marked where all the best fishing spots are. And if we can put the pieces together like a puzzle, maybe . . ."

". . . we can help Dad catch the big one!" said Devin.

"Yes!" said Ethan. "This is going to be Dad's year. I can feel it."

And all thanks to Mystic, he thought, reaching over to scratch the pup's head.

CHAPTER 4

Ethan spun the scrap of paper around in his hand and studied the map that he and his friends had been piecing together on the ground. They'd been at it for fifteen minutes now, but it was slow going.

He sat back on his heels. "This is really hard. It's like trying to put together a puzzle without all the pieces."

"And no box, so we can't even see how it's supposed to look when its finished!" said Devin, sounding just as discouraged as Ethan felt.

When Dad wandered over, Ethan barely noticed, he was so into the puzzle. "Whatcha doing?" Dad asked, leaning over.

"Trying to solve a puzzle," said Carlo, holding up a piece. "We found part of a fishing map."

"Oh," said Dad, studying the piece. "Does it look like this one?" He pulled something from his pocket: a smooth, crisp, freshly folded fishing map.

The *same* fishing map.

"Yes!" said Ethan, blowing out a breath of relief. "Where did you get that?"

Dad pointed toward the information center— the giant wooden sign near the parking lot. "There are about a hundred of them in a box near that sign. Free for the taking. Do you want me to go get you one?"

"No," said Devin. "Those aren't exactly like this one. *This* one has a secret code on it."

"Sounds mysterious," said Dad. "What kind of code?"

"A Magikarp Code," said Ethan. "Or at least a fish code. We think it might tell you where to catch the big one, Dad."

Dad's eyes lit up like a kid in the candy shop. "Well, in that case," he said, "how can I help?"

An hour later, Ethan and his friends had found

every piece of the map that had the Magikarp Code drawn on it. And they'd taped those pieces over the matching parts of Dad's new map.

It wasn't perfect. They'd had to use the lure tape from Dad's tackle box, which was sparkly and kind of distracting. But now they could clearly see which parts of the map were coded with groups of fish.

"I'm pretty sure the places with three fish are where we want to start fishing," said Gianna.

"What do you mean we?" asked Carlo.

"I'm going to help Ethan and Devin's dad!" said Gianna. "Maybe I can be the navigator."

"Great!" said Dad, nearly bubbling over with excitement himself. "We could rent a boat." He nodded toward the racks of aluminum fishing boats near the boat launch. "It'll be fun."

Ethan's stomach suddenly flip-flopped with nervousness. Sometimes when Dad used the words *It'll be fun*, he jinxed whatever they were about to do.

But the big one was out there waiting somewhere. *So if Dad needs help,* Ethan thought, *I'm in!*

The fishing boat had two seats and two oars. Ethan

and Gianna squeezed together on one seat, while Dad rowed from the other.

"Are you sure you don't want to come?" Gianna called to Carlo, who had decided to stay onshore.

He just tossed his hair and shook his head. He was already hunting for Pokémon.

But Ethan thought Devin looked pretty disappointed as the boat left her behind onshore. She lifted Mystic's paw and gave a tiny wave.

NO DOGS ALLOWED IN BOATS. That's what the sign at the rental counter had said. So Ethan had agreed to trade places with Devin after a half hour in the boat. He was secretly hoping that Dad would have bagged his Northern by then.

"Where to?" asked Dad, glancing over his shoulder at Gianna. She had the taped-up map spread out on her lap.

"That way," she pointed. "Toward the reeds. That's a three-fish zone."

Dad rowed hard, zigzagging toward the reeds. By the time they reached the marsh, he was out of breath. But he dropped the anchor into the water with a smile. He hummed while he chose his lure, and did a little dance as he cast his line over the side of the boat.

Then they waited.

Ethan stared at the bobber for so long, he

started to imagine that maybe it had moved—at least a little.

But Gianna assured him that it had not.

Time ticked down on the stopwatch Ethan had set on his phone. Ten minutes left, then nine minutes, then eight . . .

Finally, it happened. The bobber dunked under the water and popped back up.

"You've got a bite!" shouted Gianna.

Dad quickly reeled in the line, smiling from ear to ear. "It feels heavy," he said. "This could be it!"

Ethan held his breath and watched the line grow taut. Whatever was on the hook was fighting. *Hopefully it's not a carp*, he thought.

It wasn't.

The little orange fish that broke free from the water looked more like a *goldfish*. But Ethan wasn't going to be the first one to say it.

"What's . . . that?" asked Gianna.

Dad sighed. "A Pumpkinseed," he said. "The perfect pan fish."

The only person who was even remotely excited about the Pumpkinseed was Devin. When they got back to shore to pick her up, she admired the orange fish—and then compared it to Mystic.

"I'm going to call *you* Pumpkinseed," she said to Mystic as she handed the puppy's leash to Ethan.

"Because you're little, orange, and loveable."

Ethan tried to hide his irritation. But as soon as Devin was on the boat and out of earshot, he said, "Her *name* is Mystic."

Carlo laughed from a few feet away. "Got it," he said. "I just got a Poliwag, too—one of those tadpole-like Pokémon. The rocks over here are crawling with them!"

"Whatcha catching?" a voice called from the bridge up above. "Tadpoles for bait?"

It was a fisherman—the one with the bright white hair that Ethan and Devin had seen yesterday.

"Not real tadpoles," Carlo explained. "Poliwag. Pokémon."

The man nodded, but Ethan was pretty sure he had no idea what Pokémon were. *There are people here catching fish, and people here catching Pokémon. But there aren't a lot of people doing both*, he realized.

"Can I watch you catch a Poliwag?" Ethan asked Carlo. "I'm trying to work on my throw."

"Sure," said Carlo, kneeling. "There's one now." He showed Ethan how he waited for the circle around the Pokémon to shrink about half-way down. "If I throw the ball now, I can hit the Pokémon right in the chest—when the circle is at its smallest. Then I'll get the excellent throw bonus."

He almost did, too. His throw was only slightly off. It bounced off the Poliwag's head. "Great!" said the screen.

Ethan practically turned green with envy when Carlo collected his extra fifty experience points.

"Gia is the real expert," Carlo admitted. "You should watch her new technique. She holds the phone upside down when she throws the Poké Ball!"

"No way!" Ethan spun his phone around to try to catch the Poliwag. But every time he threw a Poké Ball, Mystic tugged on the leash, and the ball flew off the screen.

Who am I kidding? I can't even throw a Poké Ball when I'm holding my phone the right way, he thought with disgust.

He finally gave up and sat back on a rock, watching the boats bob on the water and the fishermen casting lines from the bridge above. He saw kids running around the lake with their phones out, too. They were Pokémon hunting like Carlo.

When Mystic tugged at the leash again, Ethan sighed. "What?" he asked. "What's so freaking exciting?"

That's when he saw the dead worm on the nearby rock. Mystic's nose was twitching toward it as if she smelled a turkey dinner.

"Ew!" said Ethan. "No! You get into the grossest things. How am I going to teach you not to go after dead fish and slimy worms?"

Mystic wagged her tail and kissed his hand. Ethan tried not to think about everything that had been in her mouth today. Instead, he returned the kiss—on the top of her head.

Then she barked toward the boat.

When Ethan glanced up, he saw Dad standing in the boat. *What does he see? Is it the big one?* Ethan wondered.

No, Dad was looking down at something in his hand. His *phone*. Was he playing Pokémon GO?

As he took a step toward the front of the boat, he stumbled over an oar.

Ethan watched in horror as Dad tumbled over the edge of the boat and plunged into the lake below.

CHAPTER 5

"**W**as it the big one, Dad?" Ethan asked. He tried not to smile as Dad wrung out his T-shirt and hung it over tree branch.

"Yes," said Dad. "At least, that's what we're going to tell your mother. It was the biggest fish I've ever seen."

"Or the cutest little Horsea," said Devin, giggling.

"You fell overboard trying to capture a Horsea?" asked Ethan. "I was hoping it was something tough, like a Gyarados."

"One of those dragonlike Pokémon?" asked Devin. "Nope. Just a Horsea. Dad got bored when he couldn't find the big fish, so he started going after the little Pokémon."

"And I think he wrecked his phone," said Gianna.

Ethan watched his Dad shake the phone and then hold it to his ear, as if he hoped to hear it ticking, like a watch.

"Now two of us are without phones," said Gianna. She seemed pretty disappointed about that.

"How did Mystic behave?" asked Devin, changing the subject, as usual.

At the sound of her name, the puppy raced toward Devin and licked her ankle.

Ethan shrugged. "She was trying to eat a dead worm. We really have to teach her not to go after certain things—for her own good."

As he watched Dad drain the water out of his shoe, he thought, *And we're going to have to teach Dad not to go after certain things, too. At least while he's in a boat!*

"So we were wrong about the Magikarp Code," Gianna announced. "Three fish on the map does not equal lots of big fish in the area. That stinks."

"Right," said Ethan. "But this Diglett chocolate cake pop? This definitely does *not* stink." He slid the cake pop off the stick and ate it in one bite. Then he settled back into the bench. "I've missed Dottie's Doughnuts."

"It's not a Diglett. It's a Dugtrio," said Devin. "We got three of them for the price of two, remember? Good thing Carlo had to work, or we would have been one cake pop short." She licked chocolate frosting off her fingers before Mystic could do it for her. Then she gently tapped the whining puppy's nose. "No, Misty. Chocolate isn't good for dogs."

Ethan peered through the glass window into the doughnut shop, wondering what he should have next. A Clefairy with pink frosting and whipped cream filling? Or his favorite—the Mankey with banana cream filling? Dottie sure got creative when it came to making doughnuts!

As if she read his mind, Dottie hurried out the front door. "How are my favorite Team Mystic players today?" she asked. "I've missed your faces around here!" She held a bowl of water in her hand, which she set down on the sidewalk for Mystic. "I wish I could invite you inside, but puppies aren't allowed in bakeries. Health code rules."

Devin smiled as she slid the water bowl closer

to Mystic. "We understand," she said. "Mystic still smells a little bit like Magikarp, anyway. It wouldn't be good for business."

Dottie cocked her head, setting her gold earrings jingling. "A magic harp? What on earth is that?"

Devin started laughing so hard that she couldn't explain.

"It's a Magi-*karp*," said Ethan, emphasizing the second part of the word. "It's a fishlike Pokémon. Mystic rolls in dead fish when we go to the lake. She likes worms, too." He made a face.

"Hmm," said Dottie, tapping her chin. "That gives this baker an idea. How about if my next "Pokémon concoction is a Magikarp doughnut? Picture it now: a gummy tail, candy eyes . . ."

"No," said Devin, scrunching up her freckled nose. "No, no, no. Gross. I'm sorry, Dottie, but that's a bad idea."

But Mystic wagged her tail and licked her chops.

Dottie laughed. "I think that furry teddy bear of yours disagrees. Maybe I should open up a second shop and call it Dottie's *Doggie* Doughnuts." She winked at the kids before disappearing back into the shop.

"I think she's kidding, but that's actually a

pretty good idea!" said Ethan. "I wish I had as many good ideas as Dottie when it came to cracking the Magikarp Code."

"Speaking of that, do you have the map with you?" asked Gianna. "I want to study the code again."

Ethan slid the map out of the lower pocket of his shorts and handed it to her, holding it up high so that Mystic couldn't reach it with her sharp little teeth.

"Why do you call it the Magikarp Code, anyway?" asked Devin. "We didn't catch any carp when we were using it."

Ethan shrugged. "I don't know. I guess because the fish symbols look like they're lying on their sides, like a Magikarp."

Devin leaned over the map. "You're right!" she said. "But they're a lot less floppy."

"Hmm . . ." said Gianna. "I wonder . . ."

"What?" asked Ethan.

"I wonder if you're on to something with this Magikarp thing," she said, sitting up straight. "What if the fish symbols on the map don't show where real fish are? What if they show where *Pokémon* are hidden, instead?"

Ethan almost shot down the idea. It was a *fishing* map, after all, not a Pokémon GO map.

Then he remembered something: the image of Dad going after that Horsea in the boat, right before toppling over the edge. "It's true!" he said, jumping up. "Dad didn't catch the big fish in that spot by the reeds, but he *did* catch a Pokémon!"

"Actually, he never did catch the Horsea," said Devin, giggling. "But he sure tried to. It's hard to catch a Pokémon when you're splashing around in the lake with a soaking-wet phone."

"True," said Ethan. "Speaking of Dad's drowned phone, he should be back home any minute now with his new one. Should we ask him if we can go back to the lake? I want to test out Gia's theory."

"Me, too!" said Gianna. "Maybe Carlo and I can ride our bikes there when he's done with work. Will you bring the map?"

"Yes!" said Ethan. "And the dog with the nose for dead fish. C'mon, Mystic. Let's go home and see if Dad's there."

Mystic was lying down by the water bowl. When Ethan patted his leg, she just yawned and wagged her tail.

"Seriously?" said Ethan. "C'mon, Mystic, let's go!" He tried to use a firm voice. And he started to jog down the sidewalk, hoping she'd follow. But she just rested her head on Devin's foot, as if Ethan were the most boring thing around.

"*I'll* bring the dog," said Devin, laughing. She stood up, and Mystic instantly sprang to attention. Her little ears perked up, and she cocked her head at Devin as if to say, "Where to now, boss?"

Whatever, thought Ethan, swallowing his jealousy. *I don't need a dog to catch Pokémon—not with a coded map in my pocket.*

He patted that pocket and started walking toward home. He could hardly wait to get back to the lake and start searching!

CHAPTER 6

As Dad arranged his fishing pole and tackle box just the way he liked them under the willow tree, Ethan stared at Dad's phone. He could barely see it, because it was safely sealed in a thick plastic bag.

"So your new phone is safe from the water now," said Ethan. "But how do you *use* it? What if you get an emergency phone call?"

Dad fiddled with the zipper seal on the bag. "Well then I just unzip it, like this." He tugged on the zipper, but it wouldn't budge.

Finally he used his teeth to open the protective plastic bag. "See? Presto." Dad tried to act excited, but Ethan could tell he was pretty bummed.

No more Pokémon GO playing at the lake for Dad, he thought. *But it's time for Devin and me to get started!*

When he saw two bikes heading across the parking lot, he nudged his sister. "Gia and Carlo are here. Let's go!"

Mystic raced toward the bikes, barking happily. She seemed used to Gianna and Carlo now—they weren't strangers to her anymore.

"Hey, little lion," said Gianna as she pulled her bike into a rack. She leaned over to scratch Mystic's orange "mane."

"Little Lion—I like that!" said Devin. "That's what we'll call you today. You're my little lioness." She crouched beside Mystic, who licked her face.

Ethan stuck his fingers in his ears. *La, la, la, la, la . . .* Until Carlo said something. "What's that?" asked Ethan, removing his fingers.

"I asked if you have the map," said Carlo. "Gianna said we were going to use it to hunt for Pokémon today."

"Yes! Right here." Ethan slid it out and unfolded it carefully, hoping the coded pieces of paper would stick to the map and not to each other.

They spread it out on a patch of flat grass. "Okay," said Carlo, "so we have three fish by the reeds, where your dad fell in. We know he spotted at least a Horsea there. And there are three fish over here, too, by the boat launch. And another three by the dogs' swimming area, way over there." He pointed past the beach, toward the long pier.

"Let's look by the boats first," said Gianna. "I have a good feeling about that spot."

Devin had her phone out—she was armed and ready. But as soon as Mystic started tugging on the leash, she handed her phone to Gianna. "You search first," she said. "I've got my hands full already."

Ethan almost offered to take the dog from her. *But why bother?* he thought. *Mystic doesn't listen to me anyway.*

As they hurried toward the boat launch, he kept his eye on the tracking feature in the lower corner of his phone. "If we're right about this, we'll start seeing Pokémon any minute now," he said.

C'mon!

Come out, come out, wherever you are!

But his tracking box stayed empty. By the time they were standing next to the rack of rental canoes and kayaks, the only thing showing up in Ethan's box was a Weedle.

"Go away, Larry," he muttered. Then he shook his head. "Something's not right. Let's try the other three-fish spots."

Mystic led the way, jogging toward the dogs' swimming area.

"Keep a hold of her," he warned Devin. "If she sees a tennis ball, she's going to go nuts."

"I will," said Devin. "She listens to me, remember?"

Ethan's cheeks burned. What Devin said was true. But did she have to point it out in front of everybody?

Focus on the Magikarp Code, he reminded himself.

The three fish on the map were near the end of the long pier in the dogs' swimming area. As they got closer, Ethan could see that there weren't any dogs in the water today. That was a good thing— maybe Mystic wouldn't go nuts this time and try to break free.

He followed Gianna and Carlo all the way out to the end of the pier.

"Hang on to your phone," said Gianna. "You don't want to have to carry around one of those ziplock phone-baggy things like your dad."

She grinned at him, but Ethan couldn't smile back. Because the tracking feature on his phone was empty. *Totally* empty.

"Where are all the Pokémon?" he asked.

"There aren't any," Carlo confirmed. "None.

Zilch. Nada." He leaned against the post at the end of the pier.

Gianna sighed. "I guess I was wrong," she said. "I hate it when that happens."

"It's okay," said Devin. "The boys were wrong about the code, too, when they thought it showed where all the big fish were."

Ethan glared back at her, ready to argue. Why did she have to point out everything he did wrong today?

But before he could snap at her, Mystic started yapping at something. Two Labrador Retrievers were racing toward the water. And just like before, they were fighting over a muddy tennis ball.

"Grab Mystic!" Ethan said to Devin.

She had a hold of the dog's leash, but Mystic caught sight of that ball and immediately took Devin for a quick and jerky jog down the pier.

When Mystic reached the Chocolate Lab, she stood up on her hind legs and snatched the tennis ball—right out of his mouth! Or she tried to, anyway. It was too big for her own mouth and bounced onto the ground below.

"Mystic," said Devin, scolding her. "That was naughty. That ball isn't yours."

The Chocolate Lab seemed to agree. He scooped up the ball in his own, much bigger, mouth. Then he backed away from Mystic, growling. Ethan couldn't tell if he was challenging her to a friendly game of tug-of-war or warning her to stay away.

"C'mon, Snickers," called a boy jogging down the trail toward the water. "Bring it to me." It was the same kid they had seen their first day at the lake.

The one who was kind of annoyed with Mystic, Ethan remembered.

He watched as the dog brought the tennis ball to the boy and dropped it at his feet.

"What a good dog!" said Devin. "I wish we could train Misty to do that."

"We forgot to bring her tennis ball with us, *again*," said Ethan, slapping his forehead. "We were going to do that, remember?"

But as they left the pier and walked past the boy and his retriever, Ethan had a sinking feeling in his stomach.

Why bother with the ball? I'm never going to be able to train my dog to retrieve it, he thought. *Devin might be able to. But I won't.*

He trudged behind Carlo and Gianna, all the way back to the Badfish Creek Bridge.

"So we were wrong about the Magikarp Code," Carlo recapped as they walked. "And it looks like we were wrong about the Magikarp Kid, too." He stared at his phone. "That trainer is back, and stronger than ever."

"What?!" Ethan pulled out his phone. Sure enough, the Badfish Creek Bridge gym was Team-Instinct yellow again. "But how?"

"He's got a friend with him this time," said Carlo. "A Defender named Sandstorm with a Kingler. And take a look at what Magikarp Kid is fighting with."

Ethan looked for the Magikarp. But the Magikarp Kid wasn't using that carplike Pokémon anymore. He had upgraded. He was battling with a *Gyarados* now.

"No way," said Ethan, staring at the blue, dragonlike Pokémon spinning at the top of the gym. It looked fierce. "Did he evolve a Magikarp?"

Devin shook her head. "That takes like four hundred Magikarp Candy. Nobody could ever catch that many!"

Carlo shrugged. "Maybe someone who lives around here could. Or the kid caught it in the wild, or hatched it from an egg. I'm not sure. But I don't know if I can fight that Pokémon and win. We're going to have to think about what types of Pokémon are strongest against it."

Ethan tried to think. "Gyarados is a Water-type

Pokémon, right?"

Carlo nodded. "But it's a Flying type, too. Grass- and Electric-type Pokémon are effective against Water types. And Electric types are also really effective against Flying types, so . . . we should check our Pokédexes for Electric-type Pokémon. My Jolteon, Sparky, would be a good choice."

Devin sucked in her breath. "How do you know all that, Carlo—about the types?"

He shrugged. "Just practice, I guess. The more you fight, the more you'll remember." Then he grinned and said what he often said. "Stick with me, kids."

Ethan scrolled through his Pokémon, searching for an Electric type with high Combat Power. All he had was a Voltorb, but it would have to do. He added it to his five toughest Pokémon and crossed his fingers that it would drain the gym of at least a few prestige points.

Gianna had a Pikachu she was able to power up, so Devin let Gianna use her phone for the battle while she hung on to Mystic.

And then the battle was on.

Ethan's Meowth was up first against Kingler, the crablike Pokémon. "Ready, set, go!" Ethan whispered. He dodged Kingler's first attack and then started tapping the screen as fast as he could. Then his fingers slipped, and the phone nearly jumped out of his hand.

"Oops!" Ethan's Meowth was down before it could even perform its Body Slam.

"C'mon, Vaporeon," said Ethan, readying his next Pokémon for battle. He held the phone firmly in his hand this time and tapped until his finger started to hurt. "Water Pulse!" he ordered.

Vaporeon listened much better than Mystic. Kingler took the hit, but came back with its claws snapping. It performed a Water Pulse, too. Ethan tried to dodge, but he was too late.

"Ouch. I did not see that coming," Ethan said under his breath. He'd forgotten that Kingler was a Water-type Pokémon, too—with higher Combat Power than Vaporeon.

By the time Kingler delivered its Metal Claw attack, Vaporeon's health bar was in the red.

Poof!

Vaporeon disappeared.

So did Poliwhirl a moment later.

And Kakuna.

When Voltorb took the ready position, Ethan was sweating. "C'mon, Voltorb," he whispered. "You're my last hope!" The Pokémon looked like a wobbly Poké Ball, shaking with anger and the excitement of battle.

"Get that Kingler!" shouted Ethan, his fingers tapping the phone so hard he could barely see the vibrating screen.

He heard Devin scolding Mystic next to him, but he tried to stay focused.

As he held his finger down on Kingler's crabby face, Voltorb sent a spark flying across the screen.

"Mystic, stop!" Devin hollered.

"Devin, be quiet!" Ethan hollered right back. "You're distracting me!"

By the time he turned back to his game, Voltorb was gone.

Poof!

"Devin!" Ethan cried. "You made me lose. I never even got the chance to fight Gyarados!"

But his sister wasn't listening. She was trying to wrestle something out of Mystic's mouth.

Is that a newspaper? Ethan wondered. Then he saw the swirly blue and green shapes—and the bright red ink. That was no newspaper. *That* was a map.

Another fishing map.

Another *coded* fishing map!

CHAPTER 7

"Sheesh, what's all the commotion about?" asked Gianna, lowering her phone. "How's Giadude99, expert Pokémon Trainer, supposed to get anything done around here?"

By the annoyed look on her face, Ethan could tell that she had lost the battle against Team Instinct, too.

Then she caught sight of the map. "Is that what I think it is?"

Devin nodded—and finally managed to coax the map out of Mystic's mouth. "She found it stuck into the bridge rail. I think it has codes on it!"

When a tan, teenage boy with a fishing pole

glanced over, Devin lowered her voice. "Should we take it somewhere else?"

"This way," said Carlo, gesturing toward shore.

They met by the rocks below the bridge, the same place where Carlo had caught a whole school of Poliwag yesterday. Then they spread out the map on a wide, flat rock.

This map was coded a lot like the old one, Ethan noticed. There were three fish by the reeds. Three fish by the dog-swimming pier. One fish drawn by the beach, and one more by the picnic area.

"But look what's new," said Carlo. "Here are two fish, right by the rocks."

"These rocks?" asked Ethan, looking down at the ones they were sitting on.

Carlo spun the map around. "Yeah," he said. "These rocks. Weird."

Ethan glanced around to see if there were any fishermen nearby. The teen boy was still fishing from the bridge, but he was the closest one. "This doesn't exactly seem like a hot spot for fishing," said Ethan.

"How about for Pokémon hunting?" asked Gianna, sliding Devin's phone out of her pocket.

Ethan checked his own phone. The first thing he saw was that the gym on the bridge was still yellow. *So Carlozard14 didn't beat Magikarp Kid either*, he realized. But Carlo was much better at hiding his disappointment than Ethan and Gianna had been.

The next thing Ethan saw was a round, blue-and-white Pokémon.

"Poliwag alert," he said, nudging Carlo's arm.

"Again?" said Carlo.

"Okay, so there are at least some Pokémon here," said Gianna, checking the phone in her hand. "But we already proved that the symbols on the map aren't Pokémon, right?"

Devin nodded. "Right."

Mystic barked up at her, as if to add her two cents. The puppy had been sticking to Devin like glue all day. Ethan could barely take it anymore.

He'd been planning to ask Gianna for some Poké Ball throwing tips today. And there was a Poliwag bobbing right there on his screen, ripe for the picking. But Ethan just didn't have the heart to play.

He dropped his phone in his pocket and slumped down on the rock. "So now what?" he grumbled. "Team Mystic lost the battle against Team Instinct, and we're pretty much blowing the Case of the Magikarp Code, too."

"Wow," said Gianna, leaning away from him.

"Complain much?"

Ethan knew he was being a downer, but he couldn't help it. He really, *really* needed something to go his way today. He avoided Gianna's eyes and picked at the rubbery tip of his shoe.

"Maybe you're just thirsty, like Mystic," said Devin. She tugged on the puppy's leash, trying to keep her from lapping up the lake water. "C'mon. Let's go get something to drink from Dad."

I'm not thirsty, Ethan wanted to whine. *I'm not your puppy, something you can just lead around. Maybe Mystic is, but I'm not.*

So when the other three hopped up and headed toward Dad and the cooler, Ethan stayed behind.

Until he realized just how hot and thirsty he really was.

Then he reluctantly pushed himself up and headed toward the shade of the willow tree.

"Crispy little fish!" Dad announced at dinner that night. "Bluegill, Sunfish, and Pumpkinseed—Devin's new favorite." He winked at Devin as he slid a crispy filet onto her plate.

Mystic whined from beneath the table, her nose sniffing like crazy.

Ethan thought about sneaking her a piece of fish. *Maybe then she'll finally acknowledge me*, he thought. But Mom had eagle eyes. She'd spot the handout for sure, and that would take this day from bad to worse—fast.

"So, did you catch the big one today?" Mom asked, smiling at Dad as she spread a paper napkin across her lap.

Obviously, he didn't! thought Ethan. Or we wouldn't be eating crispy little fish. Why even bring it up?

But Dad just grinned. His sunburned face was starting to peel, and his eyes looked puffy from getting up early to fish so many mornings this week. But somehow he still had enough energy to make up a story about the one that got away.

"It was this big, right, Ethan?" said Dad, spreading his arms out as far as they would go. "And it put up quite a fight. Fought like a carp, that Northern did. Yep. So you know what I decided? I decided to let it go. I'm going to let it live another year and get even bigger. Maybe next year, I'll reel it in."

Ethan couldn't believe how happy Dad seemed. And he'd been having worse luck than anyone this week! First the nasty sunburn. Then the falling-off-the-boat incident, and ruining his cell phone. And he hadn't even come *close* to catching the big one. But here he was, eating crispy little fish and cracking jokes, as usual.

Complain much? Ethan heard Gianna's words in his head again. And he suddenly felt like a grumpy old Voltorb.

When Mystic licked his hand beneath the table, he felt his frustration start to melt away.

"Pass the crispy little fish, please," he said to his dad. "I'm suddenly starving."

After dinner, he asked Mom if he could brush Mystic, whose fluffy coat needed daily grooming.

"You know she doesn't sit very well for that," Mom warned. "You'll have to hold her tight."

"I know," said Ethan. "I just want to try."

Mom was right—Mystic was a squirmy worm during the brushing, but Ethan stayed patient and calm. He collected a whole ball of orange fur in the brush before he finally let her run away. When she headed straight for Devin's room, he tried not to let it get him down.

Later, while he was lying on the living room rug sorting through the Pokémon he'd caught, he felt her wet nose nudge his arm. *Play it cool*, he told himself. *Don't act too excited.*

He reached his hand down casually and started scratching her back. When she rolled over, the back scratch turned into a belly rub. And pretty soon the puppy was rolling from side to side on her back, snorting and grunting.

"Does that mean she likes her belly rubbed?" he asked his mom, who was reading a book in the rocking chair nearby.

"I think it means she *loves* it," said Mom, laughing. "Take your hand away and see what she does."

As soon as Ethan stopped rubbing, Mystic nudged his hand again. So he kept at it, rubbing her little tummy while she grunted and rolled from side to side. It was so cute, Ethan laughed out loud.

Even Devin came into the living room to see what all the fuss was about. "Wow," she said, "Misty likes a good belly rub, huh?" She sank down into a chair.

Ethan expected the puppy to jump up and take off toward Devin, but she didn't. She chewed at her tail for a little bit, and then she curled up in a little ball and went to sleep. *Right beside Ethan.*

A few minutes later, she started to squirm. Her legs jerked, as if she were running in her sleep. "Devin," he whispered, "I think she's dreaming!"

Devin clamped her hand over her mouth. "So cute! I'll bet she's dreaming about catching fish."

"Or *rolling* in them," said Ethan. He tried not

to laugh each time a squeaky little bark or growl escaped from the sleeping pup.

And right then and there, he forgave her.

It's okay if you don't love me best, he decided. *I'm going to love you anyway. And I'm going to train you, too, even if it takes a really long time. You'll see.*

CHAPTER 8

Mom declared Tuesday the official take-a-break-from-the-lake day. She wasn't working, and she said Dad's sunburn needed a day to heal.

"Really?" said Dad, touching his cheeks. "I thought it was looking pretty good today."

Ethan scooted his chair closer and took another look. In the light from the kitchen window, Dad seemed to have three shades of color going on now.

The bottom of his face had turned from red to brown. The top was still white. And the line in the middle still looked pretty pink. *Like Neapolitan ice cream*, thought Ethan with a grin.

"So what should we do this morning?" asked Mom. "School shopping?"

"Ugh," said Ethan. "I'm trying to pretend that we're not going back to school next week."

"Me, too," said Devin. "In fact, I have no idea what you guys are even talking about."

She scooted back her chair, scooped up Mystic, and carried her like a baby down the hall, singing an I Love Summer song that she'd pretty much just made up on the spot.

Mom sighed. "You know who's going to be the most bummed out next week when you go back to school?"

"Me?" guessed Ethan.

"Nope. Mystic. She's going to be awfully lonely around here without you two."

"Yeah," said Ethan. "Poor girl. So we should probably take her to the lake today, while we can." He raised his eyebrows at Mom hopefully, but she wasn't having it.

"Tomorrow," she said. "You can take her again tomorrow. This morning? It's school shopping."

Ethan stuck out his lower lip, pretending to pout. But the truth was, he didn't really mind a day away from the lake. He and his friends hadn't gotten any closer to cracking the Magikarp Code.

And besides, he wanted to spend some time training Mystic today.

As he went to his room to get changed, he reached down into her basket of toys and picked up her tiny tennis ball. It seemed so little compared to the one she'd tried to steal from the retriever at the lake. The memory made Ethan laugh now.

She could be stubborn and naughty, yes. But she was a tough little thing, too. *If she were a Growlithe, she'd be my strongest Pokémon*, he thought. *For sure.*

"Is Gia here yet?" asked Devin, poking her head through the door of Dottie's Doughnuts.

Mystic strained at the leash in Ethan's hand, hoping to bust into the doughnut shop, too. But he held her back and made her sit on the sidewalk.

He heard Dottie answer no, so he took a seat on the bench to wait. Then he remembered that the bike rack nearby was a PokéStop, so he pulled out his phone to gather a few Poké Balls.

Suddenly, his phone vibrated. Mystic looked up, cocked her head, and growled.

"You see it, too, huh?" Ethan whispered, staring at the purplish-blue mothlike Pokémon. "That's a

Venomoth. And they are *not* easy to catch."

"A Venomoth? Really?" said Devin, pulling out her own phone as she walked back out of the shop. "Good thing Gia just showed up. She can help you catch it."

Ethan shot off a Poké Ball without waiting, just to see if he could catch the fluttering Pokémon on his own. But it fell way short. Catching flying things wasn't Ethan's specialty. So when Gianna locked her bike up against the bike rack, he was ready to ask for help.

"How would you catch this Venomoth, Gia?" he asked her. "I really need to work on my throws." He held out his phone to Gianna.

"Okay," she said, studying the screen. "Well, see the shadow underneath the Venomoth? Watch that to see how far away the Pokémon is. Otherwise, it's hard to tell." She flung the ball and hit the Venomoth dead center.

"Excellent!" read the screen.

"Yes!" said Devin, pumping her fist.

But then the ball cracked open and the Venomoth popped out. Seconds later, the purple Pokémon disappeared in a puff of smoke.

"No way!" said Ethan.

Gianna sighed and shook her head. "Sorry, Ethan," she said, handing back his phone.

"Sometimes a Pokémon just doesn't want to be caught. We should have used a Razz Berry to sweeten it up!"

"That's okay," he said. Somehow, it made him feel better to know that Gianna didn't catch every Pokémon that crossed her path, either.

As he slid his phone back in his pocket, it bumped against something else—the tiny tennis ball he'd been carrying around all morning. He pulled it out to show Gianna. "I've been working on another kind of throw today, too."

Mystic saw the ball and immediately started jumping and barking.

"Whoa," said Gianna. "She *really* loves her ball!"

Before Ethan could give it to the puppy, Dottie came out carrying a bowl of water—and something that looked like a cookie. It was orange and shaped like a fish, and Dottie set it down right in front of Mystic.

"Is that what I think it is?" asked Ethan, his jaw dropping.

Dottie shrugged. "I had a little free time," she said. "I thought I'd whip something up for your little buddy. I'm afraid it's tuna flavored, because I couldn't find any Magikarp flavoring at the grocery store."

Devin laughed and clapped her hands. "A Magikarp biscuit for Mystic. Dottie, you're awesome!"

"I think you *should* open Dottie's Doggy Doughnuts," said Gianna. "Mystic thinks so, too."

The puppy was tackling the biscuit as if it were a real fish. She took it in her mouth and shook it a little, then set it down and started gnawing on a corner.

"Well, you kids gave me the idea," said Dottie. "You always inspire me when you come back from Pokémon hunting. Have you caught much at the lake this week?"

Ethan sighed. "Not really," he said. "Nothing's biting at Badfish Creek." He meant it as a joke, but Dottie picked right up on it.

"Badfish Creek," she said, gazing into the distance as if she could actually see it. "My grandpa used to take me fishing there when I was a little girl. And that was a long time ago." She put her hands on her hips and grinned.

"Really?" said Devin. "Did you catch bad fish at Badfish Creek?"

"Nope," said Dottie. "We caught good fish. Grandpa told me that the creek was named by fishermen who wanted to keep their favorite fishing spot a secret. They named it 'Badfish' so that other people wouldn't want to fish there, and they'd have the creek all to themselves."

"Smart!" said Ethan. "Those fishermen were pretty sneaky."

"For sure," said Gianna. "I wouldn't have thought about doing that."

"Sure you would have," said Devin. "You're plenty smart. You're the one who's been helping us figure out the Magikarp Code, remember?"

Gianna shook her head, which sent the antennae on her bug cap bouncing. "I'm much better at capturing Pokémon than I am at cracking codes."

As Ethan watched the antennae bob back and forth, he batted a thought around in his mind. Dottie's story about Badfish Creek had given him an idea, or at least the start of one.

He narrowed his eyes, trying to focus on it. But it kept fluttering around like that Venomoth, threatening to get away.

"Ethan?" Gianna said, sounding very far away. "Earth to Ethan."

"Huh?" he asked.

"Dottie wants to know what kind of doughnut you want today."

"I haven't figured that out yet," he admitted. "But I might have just figured out something else."

"What?" asked Devin, her eyes wide.

"The code," he said. "I *might* have just cracked the Magikarp Code."

CHAPTER 9

Ethan was sure Wednesday would never come. But, finally, morning sunlight spilled through the cracks in his blinds, and Dad tapped gently on his door.

Dad was all dressed and sporting his new fishing hat, which had an extra-wide brim. "Get up, lazy bones!" he sang. "Early bird catches the fish—or something like that."

Ethan sprang out of bed and hurried to get changed. Team Mystic was meeting at the lake in one hour to test his new theory about the Magikarp Code. He was half excited, half terrified. What if he was wrong?

He knew his friends would forgive him, even if he was wrong. He just really hoped he wasn't.

Devin got ready quickly, too. And she had just as much trouble finishing her cereal as Ethan did. "I'm not hungry," she finally said, pushing the bowl away. "I'm too excited!"

Beneath the table, Mystic seemed excited, too. Maybe she had seen Ethan slip her tennis ball into his pocket again today. Or maybe she could smell the extra Magikarp biscuit that Dottie had given him and Devin. That was in his pocket, too.

If Mystic wouldn't listen to him today, he'd try giving her a bit of the Magikarp biscuit. *To sweeten her up*, he thought. *Just like giving a Razz Berry to a Pokémon.*

Finally, it was time to hop in Dad's car and drive to the lake. Ethan had a feeling Gianna and Carlo would already be there, and he was right. Their bikes were locked in the rack in the parking lot by the lake.

Ethan was racing down the trail before Dad had even collected his tackle box from the trunk.

"I hope you catch the big one today, Dad!" Devin called over her shoulder.

Mystic ran at their feet, barking excitedly.

"Where are Gia and Carlo?" asked Devin, her head swiveling from side to side. "By the bridge?"

Ethan shrugged. "They probably went straight to one of the one-fish spots on the map," he said. "The beach or the picnic area."

Devin stopped running. He could almost hear the *screech* of her feet on the trail. "But we can't go there!" she said. "Those areas are off limits for dogs."

"I know," said Ethan. "We'll figure it out. Let's just get close enough to see if Gia and Carlo are there."

They walked toward the beach first, ducking around the No DOGS ALLOWED sign and keeping Mystic on a short leash. When she tugged too hard, Ethan made her sit and then fed her a bite of Magikarp biscuit.

"Are we going to get in trouble?" asked Devin, slowing to a crawl.

Ethan shrugged. "Not if we keep her under control. Wait, I think I see them. Is that Gia's bug cap?"

Something green and springy stood out from the crowd of kids on beach towels. It suddenly popped up and started bobbing toward them. Sure enough, there was Gia's smiling face, jogging closer. She met them just beyond the beach, where the grass was still green and dogs were still allowed.

"We couldn't wait to get started," she said, her eyes flashing. "And Ethan, I think you were right! The beach and the picnic grounds are both *crawling* with Pokémon. Someone set a lure at the refreshment stand. Carlo already caught a bunch of Magikarp, plus a Staryu, a Psyduck, and a Seel." She counted them off on her fingers.

"He caught a Seel?" asked Ethan.

"Yep," said Gianna. "And all in the last twenty minutes. Carlo is still hunting down by the water. So you were right about the Magikarp Code."

"Wait," said Devin. "So one fish on the map means good Pokémon hunting, not bad?"

"I guess so," said Ethan with a grin. "Just like Badfish Creek. Whoever marked the code on the maps is like a Pokémon fisherman who doesn't want to give away the best spots—at least, not to everyone."

"Weird," said Devin. "So who's the fisherman? And who is he—"

"Or she," Gianna interrupted.

"Or she making the map for?" Devin finished asking.

Ethan shrugged. "I don't know. I guess we solved part of the mystery, but not all of it."

Carlo jogged toward them from the beach, smiling widely. "Good job, buddy," he said, slapping Ethan on the back. "We brought in quite a haul already this morning! I scored three Magikarp in twenty minutes."

"So I heard," said Ethan wistfully. "Did you leave some for me?"

Gianna nodded. "Sure. I'll watch Mystic so you and Devin can take a turn. But I hope you have a lot of Poké Balls. You're going to need them!"

Ethan handed her Mystic's leash, plus part of the Magikarp cookie. "If she tugs, make her sit," he told Gianna. "And reward her with a Razz Berry."

"A what?" she asked, looking at the dog biscuit. "Oh, I get it! Cute." She looked down at Mystic, who was already begging for a bite. "Okay," said Gianna, breaking off a piece of the biscuit. "I can't resist. Just one Razz Berry. Can you sit?"

Ethan smiled and raced to catch up with Devin, who was already exploring the beach.

His phone vibrated as soon as he hit the sand. And there was Seel!

Ethan tapped on the seal-like Pokémon, who started blowing bubbles—and blowing raspberries with his tongue.

"This is my lucky day!" said Ethan, tapping his items list. "And yours, too, Seel. You, my friend, get a Razz Berry."

Ethan sat on the rocks beside the lake, staring at

the map. He was fresh out of Poké Balls, but he'd collected a ton of Pokémon. He felt like a whale that had just swallowed a giant school of fish. He was full, but happy.

"So who do we think this 'fisherperson,' is—the one who made the map?" asked Gianna. She gazed up toward Badfish Creek Bridge.

Carlo chewed on a piece of grass beside her. "Do you think it's a real fisherman?" he asked. "Because that really tan kid is always there. He's leaning against the rail right now. See him?"

Ethan shaded his eyes. "I see him. But why do you think a fisherperson made the map? Wouldn't it be someone who's playing Pokémon, not looking for real fish?"

"Well, we *did* find both maps by the bridge," Devin pointed out. "So it might be someone who's there a lot."

"True," said Ethan, settling back down on the rock. But something about Devin's theory still didn't feel quite right.

Gianna had Carlo's phone. Ethan watched her turn it upside down to catch a Poliwag.

"Can you really catch them that way?" he asked.

"Sure," she said, just as she snagged the Poliwag. "Sometimes it's easier, and it's a lot more fun, too."

Ethan couldn't turn his phone upside down to

catch Pokémon—not till he had more Poké Balls to fling. So he turned the map upside down in his lap instead.

He stared at the red fish.

"You know," he said, "maybe we're looking at this the wrong way. Maybe instead of trying to figure out who made the map, we should figure out who it was made *for*."

"Who knows?" said Devin. "Maybe it was made for us! By someone who knows how much we like hunting for Pokémon."

"But who? Like Dad, you mean?" said Ethan, glancing back toward the willow. Dad was definitely sleeping now, his hands behind his head and his legs crossed. Ethan shook his head. "No, I don't think so. We found the maps by accident, at least the first one. If Mystic hadn't chewed it to shreds, we probably never would have even seen it."

Devin rubbed Mystic's furry mane. "You're right," she said. "Mystic is the one who got us into this mystery. Now can you get us out, Misty?" When she leaned over and kissed the dog on the mouth, Ethan had to look away.

"You know she eats worms, right?"

Devin kissed Mystic again—on the head this time. "Don't listen to him," she crooned right into the puppy's ear.

"Okay, time out, you two," said Gianna, holding her hands up in a T shape. "Devin just gave me an idea. Maybe the map wasn't made for us, but it was made for someone like us—someone who likes to catch Pokémon."

"Right," said Carlo. "And judging by what we caught this morning, it's a Pokémon GO player who catches a lot of Water-type Pokémon."

"Like . . . Magikarp?" said Ethan.

His eyes immediately flicked toward the bridge. He saw his friends' heads swivel, too.

There was one Pokémon GO player here at the lake who not only caught Water-type Pokémon, but seemed to love them. Especially Magikarp.

"The Magikarp Kid," Ethan whispered.

CHAPTER 10

"**S**o what do we know about this Magikarp Kid?" asked Carlo. His voice suddenly sounded gruff, like a real detective interrogating a witness.

"Um, we know he really, really loves Magikarp," said Devin.

"Or at least that he catches a lot of them," said Gianna. "So maybe he lives around here."

Ethan thought about that for a while. He scanned the perimeter of the lake, looking for houses. But the park was pretty far out of town. The only houses he could see where the little cottages past the bridge—the ones that people from out of town rented for summer vacations.

"What else?" he asked. "Is the kid a phantom? Because we've never seen him battling at the gym, and yet he always manages to win it back. When does he come here? The middle of the night?"

Carlo was still staring toward the bridge. "Maybe we're looking right at him and we don't even know it," he said.

Ethan followed his gaze straight to that tan kid, the one who was always fishing off the bridge.

"You think that's Magikarp Kid?" he asked.

Carlo shrugged. "He's always there, and he likes to fish—at least, he pretends to."

"It'd be pretty hard to play Pokémon GO with a fishing rod in your hand," Gianna pointed out.

"Yeah," said Ethan. *Sometimes it's hard to battle even when you're not holding a fishing rod*, he thought, remembering how his phone had almost slipped out of his sweaty palms during the last one.

"I say we go check it out," said Gianna, and she wasted no time. She hopped right up and brushed off her shorts. "Can I borrow your phone, Carlo?" As soon as he handed it to her, she straightened out her bug cap and marched toward the bridge.

"What's she going to do? Just go ask him if he's the kid getting all the maps?" asked Ethan, shading his eyes against the sun. Sometimes he thought

Gianna was the bravest kid on Team Mystic.

Carlo shrugged. "With Gianna, who knows?" he said. "But she might need some back up."

"I'll go," said Ethan, before he'd really thought his plan through.

As he walked toward the bridge, he felt his stomach flip-flop. *What's Gia going to do?* he wondered again as he watched her lean against the rail near the boy.

She didn't talk to him right away. She pulled out her phone as if she were taking photos of the water below.

Ethan stopped at the end of the bridge a few feet away. He pulled out his own phone and pretended to play Pokémon GO. Then he heard the boy ask, "Is that Pokémon GO you're playing?"

But he wasn't asking Ethan. He was asking Gianna.

"Yes!" she answered brightly. "Do you play, too?"

Good! thought Ethan. *She's getting somewhere already.* He angled his phone and his body so that he could see Gianna's face.

"Who's your favorite Pokémon?" Gianna asked the boy. "I'm a fan of Bug types, obviously." She tilted her head back and forth until her antennae wiggled.

The teenager shrugged. "I don't really play," he said. "I like that sneezy one, though. What's his name, again? Achoo something?"

Gianna's smile froze on her face. "Pikachu? Yeah, he's cute. Well, nice talking to you. Gotta go." She turned and abruptly walked off the bridge, right past Ethan.

He had to sprint just to catch up with her.

"That's not our guy," she said, her teeth gritted and her body facing forward so that the kid wouldn't know they were talking about him.

"He's definitely not the Magikarp Kid," agreed Ethan. "I mean, who doesn't know Pikachu's name? Mom could even come up with that one— no problem."

As they neared the rocks, Devin looked up expectantly. Ethan shook his head at her. "It wasn't him."

She sunk back down to the ground in disappointment, and Mystic gave her a sloppy kiss on the chin.

"Let me have my phone back," Carlo said to Gianna.

She handed it to him, and he immediately pulled something up. "So we don't know who Magikarp Kid is," he said. "But what about this girl? Do we know who Sandstorm could be?"

He had pulled up the image of the other Defender of the Badfish Creek Bridge. Sandstorm was a trainer with brown hair pulled back into a ponytail. But Ethan could barely see her, he was so distracted by the giant Kingler that had wiped out his entire team of Pokémon in the last battle.

"Have we seen any girls with brown ponytails?" Carlo asked Gianna. "How about at the beach? Maybe Sandstorm is someone who really likes sand."

Gianna nodded. "I see where you're going with this, but . . . I just don't remember. I was too excited about all the Pokémon on the beach!"

But Carlo's question had sparked a memory in Ethan's mind.

"Wait," he said. "I think Devin and I met a girl named Sandy here. No, not a girl—a *dog*. We met a dog named Sandy. At the dog beach!"

"Oh, yeah," said Devin. "The first day we came here."

Carlo laughed. "So you think this Trainer is a dog?" he asked. "That would be a first."

"No," said Ethan, shaking his head. "But Sandy's owner was a girl—a girl with a long pony-tail. So maybe Sandstorm is—"

"Sandy's owner!" Gianna interrupted.

"Yes!" said Devin, jumping up. "Go, Team

Mystic!"

At the sound of her name, Mystic started barking.

"Follow me," said Ethan, jogging toward the dog swim area. "We're going back to the beach—the one where dogs are allowed. And where I *hope* we'll find a dog named Sandy!"

The dog beach was empty. Totally and completely empty.

Ethan sank down onto the end of the pier in disappointment.

Mystic seemed pretty bummed, too. She whined and ran up and down the pier, as if looking for her tennis ball-toting friends.

"Hold her tight," Ethan warned Devin. "Don't let her throw herself off the end of the pier in despair."

"I'm trying!" said Devin. "She's so strong, though. She really wants to play. We should have brought her tennis ball."

Ethan patted his pocket. "Wait, we *did* bring her tennis ball," he said, fishing it out. Mystic immediately sprang to attention.

"You're not going to throw it in the water, are

you?" asked Gianna.

"Of course not," said Ethan. "I'd throw it onshore, but we probably shouldn't take Mystic's leash off. Mom would kill us."

"True," said Devin.

So he rolled the ball on the ground toward Mystic, which seemed like the best compromise.

When the ball rolled straight toward her, Gianna clapped. "Excellent throw!" she joked. "A hundred extra points for you."

Devin wrestled it out of the puppy's mouth and tossed it back to Ethan.

His next throw rolled too far to the right—way too far. "Curveball!" Carlo called, chasing the ball down and then throwing it back.

Pretty soon, Devin was rating Ethan's throws, too. "That one was only 'nice,'" she said. "Actually, I'm lying. It wasn't nice at all. I think you can do better."

In between throws, Mystic dropped her front paws to the ground and barked. She was loving this! But she wasn't loving giving up the ball when it was time to throw it again.

"Here, give her Razz Berries—er, biscuit pieces," said Ethan, taking the Magikarp biscuit out of his pocket. There wasn't much left. He hoped Dottie would decide to bake more.

After Ethan's next throw, Devin broke off a piece of the biscuit, and Mystic gladly dropped her tennis ball to gobble it up.

That's when it happened. A brown blur tore in front of Devin and scooped up the tennis ball.

A yellow blur chased after it.

And then Mystic took off, too, disappearing into the trees.

CHAPTER 11

"**M**ystic!"

Ethan tore after the puppy, straight into the bushes. There was no trail here— just brambles and tree branches slapping against his face. But he couldn't let Mystic get away.

He couldn't see her, but he could sure hear her yipping and yapping after the bigger dogs, demanding that they give her ball back.

The woods gave way to a grassy field, which was easier to run through.

But Ethan groaned when he saw what was coming up next.

Sand.

The beach!

Would the dogs jump into the water? Would *Mystic* jump in, too?

Ethan was halfway across the beach before he remembered that dogs weren't even allowed there. But apparently those dogs hadn't read the signs, because they'd been here, alright. Ethan followed the paw prints crisscrossing back and forth in the sand, making figure eights around swimmers and beach towels.

As he leapt over a sand castle, a toddler with a shovel stared up at him, eyes wide.

He couldn't even stop to apologize to the kid's mother. There was no time. He had to find Mystic. Where was she?

"Mystic!" Devin and the others were calling for her, too. Ethan heard the frantic voices behind him, growing closer.

Then he heard something else: barking coming from the picnic area.

He took off running again, past yet another No DOGS ALLOWED sign.

It must have been lunchtime, because the picnic area was packed with grills and coolers, people and picnic blankets, grilled hot dogs and plates full of chips and salad. The dogs could be anywhere, following their noses from one feast to the next.

Ethan wasn't sure whether to look under the tables, around them, or even on them. But when he heard a commotion in the far corner of the picnic area, he knew just where to run.

"Sandy, stop!" he heard someone call.

It was her! The girl with the ponytail.

Right now, Ethan didn't care at all whether she was Sandstorm, the Gym Defender with the giant Kingler. He just hoped she could stop her dog so that Mystic would stop running, too.

"Sandy. *Stop!*" She said the word with such force that Ethan almost stopped running, himself.

Then he saw the Yellow Lab pop out from under a picnic table and trot toward the girl, its tail between its legs. There was no tennis ball in its mouth. And there was no Chow Chow running after it.

Ethan felt his hopes pop like a bubble at a Poké Stop. Where was Mystic?

As the girl bent down to grab Sandy's collar, he hurried toward her. "Have you seen my dog?" he asked. "A little red Chow?"

The girl blew her bangs off her forehead. "I'm not even supposed to be seeing my dog right now," she said. "My little brother was on dog duty. He was supposed to keep the dogs under control. Dogs aren't allowed here in the picnic area, you know."

Ethan almost laughed out loud. "Yeah, I know. But mine got loose, too." He described Mystic again, hoping the girl would say she'd seen her. But she just shrugged.

"Let's check the bridge," she finally suggested. "Maybe Snickers ran back to my brother, Noah. He better have, anyway, or Noah's going to be in big trouble."

By then, Devin, Gianna, and Carlo had caught up to Ethan. "Did you find her?" Devin asked, the panic rising in her voice.

"Not yet," said Ethan. "We're going to check the bridge. C'mon!"

They followed the girl with the ponytail toward the bridge. Actually, they followed Sandy the Retriever, who was leading with her nose.

She led them out of the picnic area. They ran past Dad's willow tree, where Dad was snoring in the sun. Past the boat launch. Past the Poliwag rocks. All the way to Badfish Creek Bridge.

Ethan expected the dog to lead them up to the top of the bridge, where the tan teenager was still fishing with his friends.

Instead, Sandy led them *under* the bridge, to a large flat rock where a boy was sitting. Ethan recognized him immediately: it was the blonde kid with the buzz cut and the bright orange shorts. He was the owner of the Chocolate Lab—who was nowhere in sight.

"Noah!" the girl with the ponytail cried. "Where's Snickers?"

Noah put his phone away and jumped up off the rock. "I don't know! He was here a minute ago. He must have smelled hot dogs cooking or something."

His sister sighed. "It was your job to watch the dogs instead of playing Pokémon GO," she said. "We gotta find Snickers. Oh, and it sounds like he's got a friend with him, too—a little orange Chow."

"Mystic," said Devin. "Her name is Mystic." She looked like she was going to cry.

"Yeah, I remember your dog," said Noah. "She likes to steal tennis balls."

Ethan nodded. "That's her." *Only this time, your dog stole the tennis ball!* he wanted to add. But he was pretty sure that wouldn't help matters right now.

Noah led them out from under the bridge and toward the far side of the lake, past the vacation cottages.

"If I know Snickers, he's over here somewhere," said Noah. "Follow me. Or better yet, follow Sandy."

The Yellow Lab led the group with her nose

to the ground. She led them straight to a wooden structure that had what looked like a kitchen sink in the middle of it. A stench rose to greet them from the garbage bins nearby.

"Pee ew," said Devin, holding her nose. "What is this place?"

"It's a fish-cleaning station," explained Noah. "This is pretty much Snickers's favorite place. There he is now!"

Noah jogged toward the water. And there was Snickers, rolling around in the mud—or what Ethan hoped was only mud. Right beside him, as if they were best buddies, was Mystic.

Her yellow tennis ball stuck out of the end of her mouth. She'd gotten it back after all.

"Mystic!"

As soon as Devin launched toward the puppy, Mystic took off, dragging her leash behind her.

"Don't run after her!" said Ethan. "She'll think it's a game of chase."

He stood very still and whistled for her. Then he reached into his pocket. Mystic stopped running and tracked his hand with her eyes.

As soon as he pulled the Magikarp biscuit out of his pocket, she dropped her ball and hurried over.

And then she did something she'd never done

for him before.

She *sat.*

"Wow, what a smart puppy," said Noah's sister. "You trained her well."

Ethan's ears burned with pride. "Thanks," he said. Then he reached down and grabbed Mystic's leash. Firmly. As if he'd never let it go again.

Noah had a hold of Snickers's collar, too. With his other hand, he waved at Ethan. "I never introduced myself," he said. "I'm Noah."

"Yeah, I know who you are," said Ethan with a smile. "You're the Magikarp Kid."

CHAPTER 12

"How'd you know my Trainer name?" asked Noah. "Have we battled before at the gym?" Ethan was almost embarrassed to say yes. He was glad when Carlo stepped up to introduce himself.

"You've got a really powerful Gyarados," Carlo said. "I couldn't beat it. And believe me, I tried!"

"Thanks," said Noah. "It's new. It took me all summer to collect enough Magikarp to evolve it."

"That's a lot of Pokémon GO playing," said his sister, rolling her eyes. "But I shouldn't judge. I'm kind of addicted, too."

"Are you Sandstorm?" Gianna asked the girl,

with a sideways glance and a smile. "Because if you are, you're really good, too."

"Yes!" said the girl, with an embarrassed laugh. "And thanks. But you can call me Nina."

Ethan wanted to compliment her on her Kingler, but he had more pressing questions to ask.

"So why exactly do you love Magikarp so much?" he asked Noah as they walked back toward the bridge.

Noah laughed. "I don't, really. But there are lots of them to catch around here. And Snickers loves his carp. I'm pretty sure that's what he was rolling in back by the fish-cleaning station."

Ew. Ethan slowed down to put a little more distance between Mystic and the Chocolate Lab.

Then Devin asked the question that everyone was wondering. "Who made the maps showing where to find all the Pokémon?"

Noah stopped walking and shot a glance at Nina. "Did you tell them about the maps?" he asked.

She shrank back, looking offended. "No! I thought you were hoarding them all. I haven't seen a single map all week."

"That's probably because we found them," explained Gianna quickly. "At least two of them. But we weren't looking for them! Mystic here just has a knack for finding them—and chewing them up."

Noah's eyes widened. "Well that explains it!" he said. "I thought Grandpa Joe was just getting bored with the game."

"Grandpa Joe?" asked Ethan.

"Yeah," said Noah. "He's the one who made the maps for me. He'd overhear kids finding Pokémon while he was fishing, and then he'd mark down the hot spots for me and leave a map in a secret spot. It's just more fun than showing me the spots himself. It was our game this summer."

"Cool," said Ethan.

"Yeah, I wish I had a grandpa like that," said Carlo.

Noah's cheeks turned pink. "He loves to fish. When we came to the cottage this summer, he really wanted me to like fishing, too, but . . ."

"But you don't?" said Carlo. "I get it. I don't really like it either!"

Noah looked relieved. "So the maps are kind of our way of fishing together—me and Grandpa Joe."

Ethan nodded. "That's pretty cool."

When they reached the bridge, they fell into an awkward silence. "Well," said Ethan, "we'll probably see you here again tomorrow. We'll be here all week, at least until school starts."

Noah sighed. "Not us. We're packing up and going home tomorrow. Maybe we'll see you again next summer, though?"

Carlo laughed. "That'll give us time to power up our Pokémon," he said. "So we can take on that Gyarados of yours."

"For sure," said Noah with a smile. "We'll be back. C'mon, Snickers. Let's go get you a bath."

As he and Nina led the dogs toward one of the vacation cottages, Mystic strained at the leash, wanting to follow her new friends.

"I know," said Ethan. "You just made some puppy pals, and now you have to say good-bye. But the tennis ball—and the treats—are heading this way." He held out the ball, and Mystic immediately followed.

"Do you think Dad is still sleeping?" asked Devin. "He missed all the excitement!"

"I hope he's not sleeping," said Ethan. "His face was in the sun."

"Uh-oh," said Devin. She started walking a little faster.

But when they got within sight of the willow tree, they saw that Dad was talking to someone. The two men were sitting safely under the shade of the tree. *Phew!*

Ethan immediately recognized the fisherman. *I'd be able to spot that white hair from a mile away*, he thought to himself.

Dad was laughing with the man when the kids approached. "Oh, hey!" he said. "These are the kids I was telling you about. They're good kids, every one of them—mostly." He winked at Ethan. "They're not big on fishing, though."

The white-haired man smiled. "Just take them to the secret spot I showed you," he said to Dad. "Once they see what's biting there, they'll get hooked—no pun intended."

Dad laughed, of course. *That joke is right up Dad's alley*, thought Ethan. *No wonder these guys get along.*

Then Dad held up a fishing map for everyone to see. "My new fishing buddy shared a secret," he said. "X marks the spot—the spot where I'm going to catch the big one."

"Really?" said Ethan, searching the map for the X.

There it was, in the farthest corner of the lake, near the vacation rentals. The X was big. Bold. And very red.

"Grandpa Joe?" said Ethan, glancing toward the white-haired man. "Hey, are you the Pokémon map maker?"

He watched the man's face spread into a slow smile.

"That's me," said Grandpa Joe, extending a hand. "Nice to meet you."

CHAPTER 13

"He stole that information from us!" said Ethan, still thinking about Grandpa Joe. "Remember when you were catching Poliwag on the rocks, Carlo? And he asked if you were catching tadpoles? He was fishing for information about Pokémon! And we didn't even know it. That's one sneaky fisherman."

"He didn't steal information. We *gave* it to him," said Carlo with a smile. "Besides, he gave us information, too. Think about all the Pokémon I caught at the beach the other day."

"He gave me good info, too," said Dad, casting his line over the edge of the boat. "Let's hope it pans out. Actually, let me use a different word. Let's hope it's the biggest tip of the year!"

They'd rented another fishing boat—bigger this time. Gianna was navigating with the map from a seat up front.

Devin still stayed behind on shore, but she and Mystic were playing ball this time instead of watching and waving. Ethan smiled with pride when he saw Mystic sit for her ball. Devin rewarded her with the last crumbs of the Magikarp biscuit.

Then he turned to Carlo, who was sitting beside him. "Are there any Pokémon out here?" he asked.

Carlo shook his head. "But I think that's a good sign. Places that are full of Pokémon don't seem to be full of fish. And vice versa. I think we're finally figuring this place out."

"It's about time," said Ethan, peering over the side of the boat. Just as he looked down, something swam under the boat. Something long. Something dark and shadowy.

"Either that was Gyarados," he whispered, scarcely breathing, "or Dad is about to catch the big one."

"You caught the b-i-i-i-g-g one! You caught the b-i-i-i-g-g one!"

Ethan and Devin danced around Dad, repeating one of Devin's made-up songs.

Dad joined in, too, singing his own kind of lyrics as he balanced the plate of grilled fish in his hands. "I caught the b-i-i-i-g-g one. I really d-i-i-i-d-d it." He shimmied his shoulders and wiggled his hips, doing a circle dance around the dining room table.

"No crispy little fish tonight," said Mom with a smile. "Grilled Northern and homemade coleslaw. I hope you kids are hungry!"

"Starved," said Ethan. "But before we eat, I think we should all take a moment to admire Dad and his prized fish. Devin, cue the photo, please."

She tapped on her phone and scrolled through her photos. "There he is!" she said, tilting the phone so everyone could see.

Sure enough, there was Dad, holding up his Northern Pike beside him—the one that *didn't* get away. It was forty-six inches long, according to Dad. It stretched from his sunburned nose down to the bottoms of his baggy cargo shorts.

Dad's smile looked about forty-six inches wide, too. *Sunburn or no sunburn, that's one happy Dad*, thought Ethan.

"So where did you catch this again?" asked Mom, scooping coleslaw onto Dad's plate.

"I can't tell," said Dad. "It's top secret. But let's just say that I had a little help from my new friend, Joe."

"Joe?" said Mom. "Wait, is that a nickname for one of your Weedle?"

"No!" said Devin, busting out laughing. "He's a real guy."

"With a real grandson who loves Magikarp— or at least his dog does," added Ethan.

"And he has a Gyarados," said Devin. "A super-powerful one."

"Never mind," said Mom, holding up her hand. "Pokémon information overload. But speaking of dogs, where's our Mystic?"

Ethan spun around in his chair, searching. He finally found the orange fluff ball under the rocking chair, curved into a C shape. "There she is," he whispered. "She looks like a fuzzy-wuzzy caterpillar."

Her body jerked a little as she chased her own big fish, or maybe a tiny yellow tennis ball.

"Fuzzy Wuzzy," said Devin. "There's a new nickname."

This time, Ethan didn't argue. Devin could call the dog whatever she wanted. Because now he knew that when he called Mystic, his puppy would come.

Do you Love pLaying Pokémon GO?

Check out these books for fans of Pokémon GO!

Catching the
Jigglypuff Thief

ALEX POLAN

Following Meowth's
Footprints

ALEX POLAN

Chasing
Butterfree

ALEX POLAN

Cracking the
Magikarp Code

ALEX POLAN

Available wherever books are sold!